AF586511

## About the Author

Dreena Collins lives in the Channel Isles. She has been published on numerous websites and within collections, including the Bath Flash Fiction Award and Reflex Press annual anthologies.

Dreena has published two story collections, The Blue Hour and The Day I Nearly Drowned – contemporary short stories exploring challenges such as family break-up and loss. She has a third collection of flash fiction: Bird Wing.

She is a social media geek (though she hasn't mastered Tik Tok yet). Find more of her work (and general warblings) at any of the following:

http://dreenawriting.co.uk
www.facebook.com/dreenawriting
www.instagram.com/dreenawriting
Twitter: @dreenac

**ALSO BY**
**Dreena Collins**

Collected (The Complete Short Stories)

Bird Wing (A Flash Fiction Collection)

The Day I Nearly Drowned (Short Stories Vol. Two)

The Blue Hour (Short Stories Vol. One)

*Available in all territories*

# Taste

Six of the Best

Dreena Collins

First published in 2021

ISBN: 978-1-9993735-9-7

Cover design by Dreena Collins

Silhouette art modified from images appearing at:
www.clipartqueen.com

# Contents

## Little Gems and Riches

*The opening story from The Blue Hour, my first collection. Part two of this story appears in The Day I Nearly Drowned.*

Arthur walked past me, carrying a cup of tea, flickering, tremoring – the mug ready to turn as a shooting star. He made it to the sideboard and placed it down (too heavily) on a coaster beside me.

'Humph,' he said. He did not look at me.

He turned back to make the long journey to the kitchen again. He shuffled in his pyjama bottoms, feet poking out from open slippers, nails and toes both peeling like baby snail shells. This was the indignity of having to move.

By the time he had found his way back to me, he had left a trail of tea splatters on the carpet and he was red – crimson - in the face.

'There we are, then,' he said, with his gruff affection. He waved his hand as if to pat me on the leg. 'There we are.'

He took a sip of his tea. I could see it was too strong, and it looked to me as if it was made in the cup, not the pot. It put me off glancing at my own. I didn't want him to think me ungrateful. I knew what it had taken him to make it.

'It's nice to see you,' he stated, 'Nice when you come around. You know.'

He took a deep swig. It must have been too hot. Would have burnt his mouth, I was sure.

We sat for a little while in silence. I could feel the weight of his body on the couch, almost pressed against me, shifting the cushions, and warming me up. He was quite close; I liked it. I could even smell the tea on his breath.

After a little while, he shuffled himself upright. He rocked his body back and forth, long arms pressed down hard into the sofa cushions - an octogenarian chimpanzee - until he finally swung into an upright position. Once upright he stood for a moment. He swayed. Then he grabbed the remote control from the occasional table and jabbed at it, to turn on the television; I knew this was for my benefit though once it sprung to life it was so quiet, I could barely hear it.

Then he was off again: an unsteady potter.

'Must get the dinner on,' I heard him mutter.

It was only half past four.

I watched him come in and out of the kitchen, back and forth half a dozen times, until on the dining table he placed two knives, two forks. A pair of coasters. Salt and pepper. Two glasses. A miniature world in binary.

'I'm making sausages,' he said, as he looked down onto the table. He sounded terse, but I knew him of old. He was proud of this little display, of this menu.

He glanced over, and I gave him a full beam of a smile. He knew I loved sausages.

'I hope there's peas,' I thought – but I didn't dare say it aloud.

He caterpillared his feet back into the kitchen again. I could almost see the static on the carpet. I tried not to look, stared at the television before me and enjoyed the clatter of the pans, the smell of the cold tea beside me.

When he was a young man, Arthur had been both delightful, and terrifying. He was terse but affectionate; steadfastly loyal and reliable - but I didn't think I could recall a time when he had cooked for me. He had developed his domesticity and skills it seemed. It seemed strange now, to see him grow so much - yet shrink so far. Strange to both wonder in awe and sorrow. The world is mercurial in that way.

I watched him each time he came out of the kitchen door but tried not to stare.

After a comfortable little while, the telephone rang. He fought with the handset and its miniature buttons, not made for old and clumsy fingers.

'Yes?' he shouted into the phone.

I chuckled inwardly. He was angry with the caller before he even knew who they were – but I knew that in truth he was angry at himself, his awkwardness, ineptness.

'Just making dinner,' he said, and then, after a pause '…what do you mean?'

He turned around to look at the clock.

'I don't care,' he stated, curtly, 'We were hungry.'

He listened further and then he was scowling.

'We... It doesn't matter. Yes. Yes… I have to go. The potatoes are on the boil,'

He started to move back towards the phone's stand, picking up his pace as he did, as much as he could, at least.

'What! Why?' he spat out, 'Ok, do what you like.'

He slammed the phone into its holder, had to jab at it several times to bring it home.

'Edward's coming around,' he muttered as he walked towards the kitchen. 'He's invited himself to dinner. Silly sod.'

It would be wonderful to see Edward again: but Arthur would not want to hear this.

He wandered back into the kitchen to tend to the food while I watched the screen, where professional chefs seemed to be cooking for professional critics in expensive but odd, modern surroundings. In the living room, I could not help but notice the thick dust on the table where the television stood – occasional lines of clarity on the glass table-top poked through it, where the remote was dropped and picked up again, daily - writing in the sand.

He came back out with another mug of tea for me. He held it high in the air, arm outstretched like a gauntlet, a prize before him. Ostentatious. When he reached the sideboard beside me, he realised there was already a mug there, and seemed surprised. He managed to pick up the cup of ageing tea with his left hand, and swapped them, dowsing his right pyjama leg as he did so. He glanced down.

'Oh!' he cried, softly, 'I must get dressed!'

And he was off again, shuffling towards the bedroom, through a door on the other side of the dining room.

I stood and stretched my legs while he was gone.

On the mantlepiece were a series of pictures; most were familiar, had been there years. Shots of Edward when he was little, one of Arthur in his fishing gear, galoshes to his knees - the picture now weathered and dark and hard to make out. There was a formal one of me and him, together, a picture that I had always hated and which I had not known he had framed. I smiled.

Between the pictures there were little gems and riches – an old lottery ticket, a toy from a Christmas cracker, a pair of dice, a scrap of torn paper with a phone number on: no name.

He came back out from the bedroom again, but he was still not dressed. Instead he was carrying out a small bundle of washing and a newspaper.

'Right then,' he said confidently, 'Gravy!'

He put the washing down at the empty end of the dining table and attempted to balance the newspaper on top. It slowly toppled to the floor. He tried to catch it but waved his arms awkwardly around him, his fingers lacing the air, ham-fisted, maladroit. He caught the edge of the paper and it continued to fall, but now even further away. He started to bend, to retrieve it from the floor, but his bend had not reached to his waist when he thought better of this and he straightened up. Instead, he kicked the paper with his flaky foot until it was hidden beneath the table. Then he walked back into the kitchen.

Tears brimmed in my eyes.

The doorbell rang, persistently. A few seconds later he came out of the kitchen, seemingly a little panicked.

'Sit at the table!' he cried.

I did as instructed. He watched me settle before he walked to the door.

The front door entered straight into the living room and so I observed him attempt to peer through the spyhole and then fumble with the chain. He opened the door, and Edward stood there, waiting, a look of benign affection on his face, with just a hint of impatience at its edges.

'Hi, dad,' he said, 'What are we having?'

'What?' Arthur said, 'I'm busy.'

'Let me in, dad. It's cold out here.'

'Should have worn a coat,' Arthur said, as he moved to the side, to let Edward pass.

'Hello, hello,' he said, and then, 'It's dark in here, dad. Haven't you opened the curtains today?'

Edward began to move around the space, gently and efficiently, tidying cushions, opening curtains and windows, turning off the television, moving the washing into the utility area, and then collecting the mugs and a couple of side plates that littered the surfaces like debris. He smiled the whole time. Said nothing. Made no judgement.

'Can I help with tea?' he asked.

Arthur was implacable. He wanted him gone. He remained stood by the front door, hands balled as fists by his side.

'Can I smell sausages? Are they burning?'

This was enough to set Arthur in motion, back into the kitchen.

Edward sat in the chair opposite me, saying nothing, but still softly smiling.

Arthur came back out, carrying a jug of gravy, filled high, almost brimming over. Edward jumped up and took it from him.

'Don't sit there!' Arthur yelled. 'I'm sitting there.'

'Ok, Ok dad. I'll move.'

He made as if to move around to the other side of the table.

'You can't sit over there, either,' Arthur stated.

'Why?' Edward asked, eyes a little narrower.

Arthur stared at him, fronted him out. His cheeks grew pinker.

'Your mum is sitting there,' he stated.

'Mum?' Edward said. He looked at me, he looked through me, perplexed.

'Yes,' Arthur replied quickly, 'She likes sausages. You can't have any. I haven't got enough.'

A pause.

'Mum's not here, dad,' Edward replied, quietly.

I stayed still and watched them, these two men in my life. Edward young, confident, lithe: unsure how to deal with his now ageing father. Arthur still held his respect and was still the head of this family. But at the same time, he was an image, a faded photograph, of his former self. This was the privilege of being allowed to grow old. The privilege and the shame.

'Yes, she is.' Arthur stated. 'She is.'

Both men stared at me, at my place, at my self, at my absence.

'No,' Edward said, after a beat, 'No, dad.' And then, 'She's away, dad. Remember? She's gone.'

I knew what he was trying to do. But at the same time, I wondered what the point of this was. Why shake it off, bring him back – why take him away from me again?

Sometimes it's more important to be happy, than it is to be right.

'See, dad…'

And slowly, gradually and mildly, he walked over to the chair where I sat, and pulled it out, tipped it up, moved it around in the air. I moved away. I started to move away.

'No!' Arthur cried. Despair.

'See?' Edward said, so carefully, so softly.

And then he sat down on it, to join his father for dinner, and in a flicker, a tremor - on a shooting star - I left them again.

## The Mirror

*Shortlisted in The Bridport Prize, 2016*

6:30 pm

It did not matter that it was a Friday night, Mum said I had to go to bed at 7 o'clock, anyway.

She had people coming around.

She was sitting at her table, putting earrings in, and looking at me, through the me that was in the mirror. Her earrings were so long and dangly they were almost touching the freckly bits on her shoulders. They were like the tassels on grandma's curtains, only gold; I wanted to touch them. They looked like they would feel like tickles on my hand.

"Can I leave my light on and read?" I asked, looking at the back of her neck, because the 'me in the mirror' thing felt a bit weird.

She paused.

"I tell you what," she said, in a strangely quiet and deep voice, not her voice, "if you're a good boy, we can move the T.V. from the spare room into yours for the night. You can watch a film."

I reached one hand out and stroked the earring, and let it fall through my fingers like water. It felt disappointingly warm and stiff. But I didn't stop.

"Your neck is really white," I said.

"Wouldn't you like that?" she asked me, turning around to face me, pushing my hand away from the jewellery as if she was irritated with my fiddling, as usual. She smelt strong, like sponge cake. And shower gel.

"Yes, please," I said, but I wondered what I had to do, to show that I was good.

Mum turned back around to the mirror, so I sat on the edge of the bed really quiet and still and straight and not talking, because I knew she would make me leave if I was annoying.

She had stuck her hair up on top of her head. Usually she had hair falling all the way down her back and that's why I don't get to see her neck very often. But she had made it stay up with hairpins and things and it was a big pile of little curls fluttering on her head every time she moved. I wondered if she had done it to make it easier to put her earrings in. She didn't usually wear big earrings.

She stopped still and put her hands on her knees. For a second, she locked eyes with herself - like she was cross and going to tell her mirror-self off - and then she shut her eyes, tight, and took a slow, very deep breath, twice. One, two. I felt nervous all of a sudden, wondering if I had done something.

She opened her eyes again and smiled at mirror-me.

"How do I look?" she said, and turned around again, standing up, holding her dress out to the sides so I could see through the top layer of the fabric, see the shiny black fabric underneath. I didn't know there were two bits of fabric there. Why did they give her skirt two types of fabric?

I considered her question carefully and looked her over, seriously. She didn't usually look this way. It felt strange, and I didn't know if I liked it or not. And I liked that she had asked me, but I didn't know how to answer.

"Very pretty, but you'll look better when you've finished your hair." I said.

She did one of those big bursts of laughter she does when she snorts a bit like she's snoring. But then she surprised me because she carried on laughing, a little singing laugh, for a long time, leaning over like you would do when you are coughing too much to breathe, but she wasn't coughing, she was laughing, laughing like I haven't see her laugh in ages, so it made me laugh, too. I felt it start unexpectedly, like a giggle in my belly that crept out of my mouth without my permission, so I put my hand over my mouth to stop it, but it kept creeping out through my fingers. So, Mum and I were both laughing together. And it felt lovely and warm. And it felt like a memory.

6:50 pm

I could feel that the hair on the back of my head was a bit wet still, from the shower. Every now and then little trickles of water fell down like an army of ants. It was creepy, so I rubbed my head hard from side to side on the pillow really fast, to make it go away.

"What on earth are you doing?" Mum said, irritated, so I stopped.

She was standing in the middle of my room, squinting at a remote control, trying to get the DVD player to work. The light from my lamp made strange patterns across the floor, like bits of glass, and her skirt was lit up brightly, but a shadow fell across the bottom of her legs. Like she had no feet. Like she was floating.

"Do you want me to help, Mum?" I asked. I could see what she was doing wrong.

She threw the remote on my bed, but she didn't look annoyed.

"I have to finish the starters," she muttered.

She leant down and kissed me on the forehead. Her necklace fell onto my chin and then slipped across my cheek as she straightened up again, cold.

"Night, monkey," she said.

"Night," I said, and wrinkled up my nose at her and her silly nickname.

7:30 pm

Mum was playing her old-fashioned music with saxophones and ladies singing about moonlight and love when the doorbell rang. I heard her scamper down the hallway to open up, and then I couldn't quite hear what she said but the man on the other side of the door gave a really loud, sudden laugh, that sounded hot and big, and made me feel strange; then they both hissed and giggled when she tried to shush him again. He must have come in, because I heard the door shut and the noise of the cars and wind was trapped outside.

7:44 pm

Uncle Tim arrived. I knew it was him because of that special ring he does and the way he calls "Wahayyyy!" when you open the door. I wanted to go down to see him, but I couldn't because Mum had made it clear I was not to go downstairs on any account or under any circumstances, whatsoever.

I snuggled down deeper under the bedcovers and curled my body into a bean shape. The TV screen looked sideways, but it was surprisingly comfortable, and safe, even with my neck twisted around in a funny position. I scrunched up against my cuddly dinosaur, tightly. I pinned the duvet down around me and I felt like I was in a giant sock; like a giant bean, in a giant pod.

8:10 pm

I tried to focus on the film, but it was hard. I was picking at the corner of my duvet and saying my six times table to myself, when someone appeared in my doorway.

"Uncle Tim!" I cried.

The fact that it was late, and the weekend, and I had to stay upstairs - but he was standing in my room anyway - made it all much more exciting than it would normally be.

He came over to the bed, grinning. He was a tall, thin man with a long, pointed face, like an elbow.

"I'm not allowed downstairs," I stated.

"What you watching?" he asked, as he came over and sat on the edge of my bed. He faced the screen,

"Uh. Cool," he said.

I didn't think he knew the film, but he said it anyway, just to be kind. He was like that.

"Does Mum know you're in here?" I asked him. I could smell him and taste him like cold air.

"Cheeky fag," he said, as he leaned into me.

I wasn't sure what he meant, but I giggled because he winked at me and used that voice he sometimes uses when he acts like we're in a gang together; when he acts like we're mates.

"Is Aunty Lynn here, too?" I asked.

"Sure is, bud," he winked again. "I'll try to get her to sneak past the armed guards too, if you like, but she's less likely to resist than I am so I wouldn't hold your breath."

"No," I said, but his words were like a tangled ball of knotted wool in my head and I couldn't untousle them to understand their meaning - though I felt disappointed, because it didn't sound like I would be getting any more visitors soon.

8:51 pm

The music was still playing, but everyone had moved to the kitchen and shut the door, and the front doorbell had been ringing for a really long time. I felt a little nervous sickiness in my stomach as I tried to decide what to do. I didn't want to leave someone outside, but I knew I wasn't meant to go downstairs. The bell rang repeatedly like a miniature scream, and every time it made me flinch, even though I was expecting it. It was like I could feel the noise on my skin, on my arms and cheeks. I wanted it to stop.

"Mum!" I called, "Muuum!"

I was nervous, and it sounded weird – like a loud voice trapped inside a quiet voice. Like a loud voice with no volume.

"Mum!" I said loudly and quickly.

I listened for the sound of the kitchen door opening, and her feet, but the sounds didn't come. I slipped out of bed and put my slippers and dressing gown on. The doorbell was still ringing, loud angry rings, quick loud rings now, so I took a deep breath and went out to the top of the stairs.

From the top of the staircase I could see the front door and a dark shadow through the stained glass at the top. Mum had stripped all the paint off the door a few months ago and I didn't like it; I thought it looked like it wasn't a finished house anymore, like we were going backwards and had only just moved in, instead of just settling down. Someone was banging on the door now, banging and ringing the bell. I started to walk down the stairs. It was only when I got halfway down that I realised I was still holding my dinosaur.

I reached up and opened the latch on the door.

"Where is he?" the woman said, looking straight past me down the corridor, taking a step into the house as she spoke.

I stood and looked up at her. I didn't know her. She had bright orange hair and red lipstick, and a big fluffy coat.

"Where is he?" she repeated, louder, looking at me this time, looking angrily at me and I felt the words on my face like a slap and my cheeks went red. I knew my cheeks were going red.

I didn't say anything because I didn't know what to do. I was distracted by the sharpness on my cheeks and I couldn't think what she might want, all I could think about was the stinging, and the fact I shouldn't be there, and she shouldn't be there.

She made a 'chuh' noise of irritation and pushed my hand out the way, the one that was still holding onto the latch, and she started to walk into the hall. Just as my arm broke free from the latch and fell down by my side, the kitchen door opened at the other end of the hallway. I could hear Uncle Tim yelling something. Then the front door flew back and slammed as a quick sudden breeze flew down the corridor. It nearly knocked the lady over, but she was in the hall by now, trapped in the hall. I was trapped in the hall with her.

All the other noises stopped for a second after the loud crash. I felt a sudden urge to cry.

Uncle Tim was in the corridor, looking confused, blinking at the woman.

"Can I help you?" he said. I didn't know if it was a cross voice or not.

She said, quietly, "Where is he?"

She was looking at the floor.

"Rose! Rose, can you come here a sec?" Uncle Tim called back in the direction of the kitchen, to Mum.

"What are you doing here, eh mate? What are you doing downstairs? Let's get you back up to bed, shall we?"

He put an arm down, around me, and he sounded like he was talking to me, but he didn't look at me, he was looking at her.

Then he kept his arm around me though he didn't actually move anywhere until he heard mum come out of the kitchen and rush towards the lady with the bright orange hair.

Uncle Tim guided me upstairs then, and I could hear mum talking to the lady, and she sounded agitated and she had lost the way she was before. She sounded stressed. And then the other man, with the booming voice, was joining in and talking loudly and I heard him say the f word, at least once. You shouldn't say the f word.

And then both mum and the man were telling someone to get out.

The door slammed hard again, but this time it was on purpose.

And then in my bedroom Uncle Tim explained that I was definitely not to go downstairs on any account or under any circumstances, whatsoever. Seriously.

9:30 pm

I wasn't going to go downstairs but I needed to go out to the bathroom. I couldn't sleep, and I needed a wee so badly it felt like a hot splinter in my tummy. I stood up and I felt like I had to bend over a bit and squash my legs together because it hurt, and I was close to having an accident.

As I went to the bathroom, I could hear mummy talking to Uncle Tim, in the downstairs hallway again. Uncle Tim sounded more serious than usual, but his voice was a little bit sloppy and he was saying something about someone being married, "for God's sake," and then Mum was shushing him and saying not for much longer, no he doesn't and it's not like that and never, didn't and lots of other 'no' words.

Then Uncle Tim burst out with: "He's got kids, for crying out loud! Why didn't you tell me, sis? What on earth are you playing at?"

And then I rushed to the bathroom because I really knew I shouldn't be listening. And I really needed to wee.

9:49 pm

My film had finished ages ago and I thought I could hear someone coming quietly up the stairs, but I wasn't sure if it was just my imagination. I squeezed my eyes shut in case Mum was checking on me and I listened as carefully as I could. There was a sound like someone hopping one or two steps at a time, lightly, and a sniff, and then I heard the door to Mum's room pushed open as the wood scraped along the thick carpet and made the sound it makes, like paper ripping. And then it was all quiet again, so I opened my eyes, thinking Mum had popped into her room for some reason - and then there in front of me, by the side of my bed, was the lady with the bright orange hair.

The black make-up around her eyes had smudged and run a little bit onto her cheeks. It was worse on one side, and she had clumps of very long, thick eyelashes stuck together so that her left eye looked a little like a squashed insect. Her lipstick had rubbed off in the middle, so it was red on the edge, but pink in the middle, with thin red lines making stripes on her bottom lip.

She sniffed again. For some reason I felt weird, but not scared.

"What's the matter?" I said.

"What's not the matter?"

I didn't know what to say to that.

"Budge over," she said, pushing her knee onto my bedding, to indicate she wanted to sit on my bed, I supposed.

"You're not meant to be up here," I stated.

"No," she said, sitting down. "There's a lot of stuff we aren't meant to do. But I guess the rule book has gone out the window."

A perfectly formed tear was rolling down the side of her nose. It seemed to get bigger as it travelled down until it pooled off her top lip. She left it there, and I wondered if she could feel it at all, and I wanted her to brush it away, but she didn't. When she spoke, it splintered into tiny drops, and some of them fell into her mouth, and others stayed on her lips. I imagined what it tasted like.

"What's your name, kid?" she asked, leaning back onto the bed, with one arm outstretched behind her. She looked like she should be relaxed but wasn't; like she was pretending to be relaxed.

"I'm not allowed to tell people that," I said.

I was a bit scared not to answer her but also proud to have remembered not to tell strangers what I was called.

She snorted.

"That must make things tricky!" she said, "How do you ever introduce yourself? What do they call you in school?"

I didn't understand what she meant. She laughed to herself.

"Never mind," she said.

The weight of her arm and her hip squashed against me and felt like a little mound of cushions, which was pleasant. And she asked me why I was upstairs and about the film I watched and about my dinosaur and if I liked living with my mum, and after a while she seemed to relax a bit and I almost forgot that she wasn't supposed to be there. She was nice. And she stopped crying.

10:04 pm

"Get me a drink, kid?" she said, "A proper drink? A grown-up drink."

"Do you mean wine?" I asked. I could feel my eyes hurting and then realised I was staring, and I wasn't blinking.

"That'll do," she said.

I knew mummy would be incredibly cross if she knew the lady was in my room and then if I went downstairs that would be even worse. But the lady still looked just a little bit sad and her make-up was still scribbly, and, in a way, I didn't want her to leave me. She was sat on my bed and it made my feet warm and also it didn't matter that I couldn't sleep anymore because she was just sat there so I wasn't on my own. She grabbed my fingers. Her hand was surprisingly cold and small.

"Please," she said.

I whispered out of bed again and out into the corridor. As I went through the door, I heard her say "Good boy," very quietly, and I smiled to myself, and I felt brave.

10:08 pm

Everyone had gone into the lounge and they were playing different music. It was fast and modern. It didn't sound like Mum's music at all. Someone's coat had fallen off the coat pegs in the hall and there was a small patch of a dark drink on the black and white tiles, like coffee maybe. I could hear loud voices but not so much laughter anymore.

I kept my head down and went as quickly as I could into the kitchen. The double doors into the garden were open, slightly. A cool breeze poured into the room like a stream, and the papers on the sideboard flickered.

There were a few plates and lots of glasses on the side, a couple of empty wine bottles and a giant beer bottle. I pulled a green plastic tumbler out of the dishwasher, which was beeping quietly, so I knew it was finished. There was a blue glass bottle and I poured some of the clear liquid into the tumbler. Then a big splash more. I grabbed a half-eaten bowl of peanuts and put it in the crook of my left arm. I walked back towards the hallway, quickly, when I spotted a man, a stranger. He was just coming out of the living room. He saw me and shut the door behind himself. He put one finger to his mouth. Sshhh.

"Midnight feast, eh?" he said in an exaggerated whisper.

He had a big head, and it was wobbling slightly. His mouth was slightly purple. I didn't like it. His shirt was unbuttoned a little bit and out the top poked some dark grey hair. Wire. His chin was slightly wet.

I didn't say anything. I walked past him quickly and up the stairs, trying not to spill the drink or the peanuts. I didn't want to look at him.

"Sorry about before!" he whispered, close to my face, as I squeezed past him in the corridor and he felt too warm, the wrong temperature.

10:12 pm

The lady with the bright orange hair took a big swig of the drink then snorted loudly, and coughed a high little cough, like a funny bird.

"Bloody hell, what is this? Vodka?" her voice was a bit too loud, "I thought you were getting me white wine!" she cried.

I was worried someone might hear.

"Sorry! I don't know! I didn't know!" I said, and I could hear my voice wailing a little bit like I was younger.

"Hey kid, it's OK You just gave me a shock!" she smiled at me, with a wonky mouth.

While I had been gone, she had done something to her face and make-up. Her left eye didn't look so bad anymore and she had red lips again. She looked very glamorous, like she should be on TV. I told her so, and she raised her plastic tumbler up in the air like people do when they say cheers.

She was asking me more questions about my mum. And she was asking me about my dad. So, I spoke to her, even told her the bits I hadn't told my friends, or my grandma, even the feelings I hadn't told my Mum, because Mum had never asked me. And she didn't seem shocked or surprised, and I felt like she understood, so I told her more and more until I had told her it all, and there was nothing left.

Then we both sat in silence for a few seconds.

She swigged her drink.

"Men are pigs," she said, "present company excepted."

And we sat in silence for a few seconds more.

"Women are pigs sometimes, though, aren't they?" I said. I felt brave to say the words but wanted to hear what she thought.

"He's incredibly selfish though," she said, "in a way that I don't think women are. I don't think any mother would do what he's done; I don't think I'd ever do what he's done."

"What has he done?" I asked.

"Run off with your mum," she stated. She looked me in the eyes. Hard. I felt ashamed.

"Sorry," I said.

"Me too," she said, softly, and she reached over to my hand again. And this time it felt warm.

She smiled, and she tipped the tumbler on its side to show me. It was empty.

"So. It's getting late," she stated. "I think I'd better go."

"Aren't you going to speak to them?" I asked.

I didn't want her to leave, though I had a feeling it might cause trouble if she spoke to mum, or Uncle Tim, or the man, so I was hoping she would say no.

"No. Suddenly doesn't seem like one of my better ideas," she said, pushing herself up off the bed and rearranging her skirt and her big furry coat.

"Well, nice to meet you," she said, sticking her hand out for me to shake.

I shook it, firmly, because that's what you do.

"How are you going to get out?" I asked her.

"Tell your mum she needs to start locking the back door," she said.

She put the tumbler on my bedside cabinet and moved towards the bedroom door, quietly, quickly. I looked up at her and stared hard at all the bits of her, in case I didn't get to see her again. I wanted to be able to remember, with her fluffy coat and her tight shiny skirt, red lips, orange hair.

"I hope things work out, you know, with your husband."

I was trying to be grown up, but I sounded awkward.

She smiled, softly, and looked a bit surprised, raising her black eyebrows slightly.

"Oh, he's not my husband, silly. He's my dad."

And then she left.

## Bird Wing

*The title story of my flash fiction collection*

The night you left us, I stayed awake until the sky woke up. The light through the curtains was a fresh bruise, stirring from black, to blue, to grey. I sat on the floor of the lounge; a bottle of wine stood proud and cold on one side – our dog lay on the other.

Towards dawn, I recall, I tried not to blink – fearful sleep or tears would conquer me. I was a warrior. I would not give in.

I moved to the sofa a few nights later. It took several weeks to make it to the spare room. When I did, I stayed on my side of the bed – considered putting pillows on yours, creating a hump to dupe my body into rest. But it was cold, inanimate: an insult to your memory.

The loss of you was a tree-stump, to trip me, to wrong-foot me, at least once an hour. Even now this happens, daily – and I am falling again. Tumbling.

Even now.

It is startling how time moves on, regardless. The calendar is splintered; whole weeks, months heaped into piles of before and after. And yet days continue to come. One after another. More and more of them, since you have gone. Mounding, piling up until this new era threatens to topple over and consume the past: to swallow my befores.

Memories, once vivid, are like a broken bird wing in decay. A crumbling moth. But I hold onto them. I box them up. They are dusty but they are mine, ours, so I keep them safe, and I preserve them as best I can.

I have become more logical in the last few months, at least. Computered. Decisive. I know I need to sleep. I know I need to use rooms the intended way: I cannot be sick in the kitchen sink. I cannot write on the walls of your study. I cannot lie across the dining table, the carcass of a beached whale – or stand in the garden, drunk, at 4 a.m.

It is not helpful to do such things.

You would be proud of me. I have started showering; I sometimes wash my clothes. I leave the house. I sleep in our room again, and Toby forms a furry lump beside me. Warm. I am not sick in sinks. I do not scrawl on walls.

And at night, I place your pillows on the floor, so they can catch me – now, yes, even now – when I fall.

## Geraldine the Powerful

*A tale of comeuppance.*

No one had ever taught Geraldine to read and write. They thought that because it was hard for her, that she wouldn't want to. Or couldn't.

But hard doesn't mean impossible.

And sometimes things that are difficult are good: like learning to ride a bike. Or learning to say: 'Worcestershire Sauce'. Or how to boil a soft-boiled egg.

Geraldine liked all those things.

She didn't remember much about school - she knew that she had gone but had a feeling that it wasn't for very long. She was at home with mum as a child, she recalled. Mum taught her numbers while they made scones. The house filled with doughy cinnamon and squidgy sultanas and they ate them warm, with butter, while they counted the raisins. Geraldine usually won, because she always ate two.

Mum told her that different doesn't mean bad, it just means different. And one day she wouldn't have to worry about anything because she would have all the money she needed and someone could take care of her, if that's what she wanted. Or she could fall in love, get married, if that's what she wanted. If that's what she liked.

Remembering mum made her feel a calmness settle across her skin. A tingle. A prickle, but a good one: it was fresh and reminded her of damp grass in the morning. Or sea mist.

Geraldine liked sea mist.

Paul said she was too stupid to learn. That it would hurt her little head. That it would tire her out. Wouldn't be good for her. Would be a waste of time. So, when mum died, so suddenly, so young, the lessons came to an end. He started giving her sheets to do on her own, but they were too tricky. How can you do what they want, when you can't read the words?

And then he gave her pictures to colour. Lots and lots of pictures. She quite liked that – she remembered shading faces blue, trees yellow, the mud red, turning the sky purple. She was magical. Powerful. But Paul didn't like that. Told her she'd done it wrong.

So, then he gave her dot-to-dot books.

And then he gave her nothing.

Geraldine was too old for school now. He didn't give her dot-to-dots for Christmas. It was her job to make the boiled eggs and toast. To put the can of soup in the saucepan. Make it hot but not too hot.

Don't let it burn and stick to the saucepan, you fool.

Then take the plates from the table and stack the dishwasher. Carefully. Do it carefully.

Paul shouted even more these days, although she tried very hard to remember to wash the white clothes on their own and to make the coffee just right. To not leave her shoes, or his shoes, in the middle of the floor. She didn't like it when he shouted. She felt it in the skin on her face, like a scold. Geraldine didn't like that.

For the last couple of years, at night, Paul had been falling asleep on the sofa after too many bottles of beer. Geraldine would take the bottles and put them in the glass bin but leave the T.V. on because the change in sound, when she switched it off, could sometimes wake him, she found. She would sneak up to her room with his tablet cradled under her arm, and let it illuminate a tent of sheets as she tapped its screen, under the covers.

She had to remember to put it back before the morning. Geraldine always remembered.

At first, she had used it to watch cartoons, and funny videos of cats. Then a few weeks later she had started to play games. That was fun.

Then one night she discovered that if you spoke into it, sometimes it spoke back. It answered her questions. Incredible. And she found that she could listen to books too, listen to words, that it could read words. Read aloud, her words. And that she could write notes and messages.

She stayed up for hours, pressing things, trying things. Getting it wrong sometimes. She often got things wrong. But she carried on.

It was a bit hard. But that didn't mean it was bad.

Geraldine's skin tingled like it was covered in sea-salt. Magical. Powerful. She watched the dark light turn to bright light around her as she stayed awake until dawn. But she did not care.

In the morning, Paul was still lying on the sofa when she came down. He was rubbing the skin on his eyes, hard. He was circling his fingers in his eye sockets. He turned, eventually, towards her as she approached him. He let his arms fall, heavily, by his side.

"I need coffee," he said.

She didn't answer, and she walked towards him, still carrying his tablet. Bold. Brave. But he had not even noticed. All those times she had snuck back into his bedroom, or crept downstairs to put it in his bag, and he didn't even notice.

"What?" he snapped, when she stood still before him.

"I've been listening to my stories," she said.

"Good for you."

"I wrote a note for you," she said.

He snorted. "Right. Well. Coffee first."

"No," she said, "Read it now. Please read it now."

She could hear her voice, up high, tight, like a little girl. A child. And louder than usual.

Like a risk.

He started to sit up.

"What the –"

She shoved the tablet in front of his face. He pushed it away, irritated, as an unwanted cat. Something to swat. But she left it there; she didn't move.

"I did it," she said. "I did it."

He sat up fully and rubbed his eyes again, then he snatched the tablet from her.

"Very good, well done," he said, before he had even had time to read it.

But then she watched his face change as he read the words, and she watched her shape change before his eyes, and she imagined that she became Geraldine, different but good, different but powerful, as he read her note.

'This is my house,' it said. 'Get out.'

## The 91 and a 1/2 Reasons Why It Can't Be True

*Winner of the Flash 500 2020 Competition, First Quarter*

You held my hand in the bar on our first date. I felt a pulse within your palm, steady and firm. For 5 minutes at a time we sat in hot, prickling silence. We didn't need to speak. We waited, pulsating, shaking. I was giddy, alive.

We drank 2 bottles of wine the next night; I tried an olive at your insistence – swallowed ½. I can still recall the taste: sour, salty, wet. We inched closer with each glass, knees knocking tables knocking knees, until you held my chin between finger and thumb, and kissed me with tears in your eyes.

You once drove 7 miles, just to be with me for 20 minutes. We stared at the clock on your phone, your arm around my shoulder, both of my hands on your knee.

When we stayed at the Bed and Breakfast, you drank 3 cups of coffee - bitter, lukewarm - and we kissed for 11 minutes before we made love for the first time.

16 grey hairs. Afterwards, you told me you had counted sixteen grey hairs, as you ran awkward fingers through the knots and kissed my forehead. You were tender. Cheeky. Curious. I laughed; planned a trip to the hairdresser.

You went away for 9 days: called me 11 times. I carried my mobile everywhere I went. I lost 4 pounds that month, floating in Merlot and a sickly, aching loss.

I bought 1 new set of bedding. It was crisp and white and optimistic. You never stayed the night.

0 lies. You told me 0 lies. You meant every word. I know it. I know it.

I know.

Because you told me that you loved me.

Twice.

## Half Moon

*Shortlisted and published by the Furious Fiction international writing competition, April 2020*

Taut, regal, she is standing on the pavement in the dark. One arm curls around a mixing bowl, the other ends in a wooden spoon. She is mixing, rhythmically. Staring into space.

It's night-time. Grandma. You need to come indoors.

She doesn't acknowledge me. Her stirring continues, batter rolling smoothly in the bowl.

The half-moon is clear, sharp, in the sky.

A car comes past, and I pull her back by her apron, in a reflex. It rides through a puddle and a wave of water lands on my left foot, just as a glob of batter falls to the ground in a splash. I look down, see another half-moon, its unsteady reflection, flickering and wobbling below.

I have forgotten my strength. She has staggered back a little onto the heels of her shoes. She trembles and then steadies herself - continues stirring.

I am close now, can smell the crisp lemon and butter in the mix.

I guide her by her elbow and we walk up the short path to the front door. My bare feet land on grit and gravel; my dressing gown flaps open a little, bereft of belt. Only underwear beneath.

She is stately by contrast. An icon. She has painted her face, her nails, her hair into an echo of herself, in hues and pigments of red. So close to what she was; so far.

Inside the house, I step in broken eggshells, granules of sugar, lemon peel. The oven is on. The kitchen table is laid for two.

What have you been up to, eh, Grandma? Why are you baking so late at night?

I take the cake mix from her, and her arms continue to move, ballroom dancing in the gaps where the bowl and spoon were. I walk her through the kitchen into the space that was, once, the dining-room. It is now her space. Photos of Grandad dot the room.

His tie is on the bed.

I lift her arms, remove the apron. I seat her on the bed and slip off her shoes. Automatically, she starts to unbutton her dress and I notice the blue ribbon of her nightie, still on, beneath it. When she is ready, I lift her legs by the ankles and slide her under the sheets. She is asleep before I leave the room. Or perhaps she was never awake.

In the morning, the sweet and acrid smell of lemons is in the air. I walk downstairs, wondering if I have managed to get up before her: thinking of tea and toast.

She is there, sitting at the kitchen table, head nodded to one side, eyes closed.

On the table are two slices of cake. Two half-drunk cups of tea. A teapot masked in a cosy in the middle. Binary. Symmetry.

I lift Grandad's tie from the crumbs on the table, and notice the teeth marks that carve semi-circles into the cake, both slices - two halves of the same moon.

## Acknowledgments

Thank you for buying my book/ checking it out of the library/ borrowing from a friend (delete as applicable: I don't mind.)

And a special thank you to Stuart, for ongoing encouragement and support.

www.ingramcontent.com/pod-product-compliance
Lightning Source LLC
LaVergne TN
LVHW052109160826
845678LV00015B/3452

*9781999373597*